LIKE NEVER BEFORE

THE UNHEARD NARRATIVE

DR. RITU SINGH

Copyright © Dr. Ritu Singh 2022
All Rights Reserved.

ISBN. 979-8-88805-496-3

This book has been published with all efforts taken to make the material error-free after the consent of the author. However, the author and the publisher do not assume and hereby disclaim any liability to any party for any loss, damage, or disruption caused by errors or omissions, whether such errors or omissions result from negligence, accident, or any other cause.

While every effort has been made to avoid any mistake or omission, this publication is being sold on the condition and understanding that neither the author nor the publishers or printers would be liable in any manner to any person by reason of any mistake or omission in this publication or for any action taken or omitted to be taken or advice rendered or accepted on the basis of this work. For any defect in printing or binding the publishers will be liable only to replace the defective copy by another copy of this work then available.

Contents

Chapter – 1

She was on her phone when he saw her coming down the stairs in a saree.

"Tsk" She looked at the strap of her sandal.

He came towards her, squatted down, kept his phone on the floor and fastened the strap of her sandal. After that, he picked up the phone and left.

She stood there mesmerised that he didn't even look at her. She couldn't even thank him.

This was their first encounter or in better words "How they met?"

"ADITI SHAH" She is always the most beautiful person wherever she goes, be it a party, school, family gatherings, etc.

She belonged to an affluent business family based in Ahmedabad, Gujarat. She had been praised for her looks since she was a kid. Some people are bestowed upon by God in every field and she was one of them.

Along with her bright persona, she had an even brighter mind and was intelligent enough to get a seat at the prestigious AIIMS, Delhi.

Now, let's introduce you to the calm and composed "VAIBHAV SINHA"; a boy with average looks but a good physique, kind and complete with a humble personality. He belonged to a small town in Uttar Pradesh and worked diligently to be at the place where he is now, AIIMS, Delhi. His father worked as a supervisor in a private factory.

AIIMS Delhi, Freshers' Party, 9:00 p.m.

"It seems you have been looking for someone," a girl asked Aditi.

"Yeah! I am," Aditi replied.

Aditi's eyes were looking for Vaibhav; the boy who had helped her with her sandal strap.

And finally, she spotted him. As she walked up to him, every eye ball turned towards her. But this was something normal for her. So, she ignored them and tapped on Vaibhav's shoulder.

Vaibhav turned back.

"Hey! Thanks for the help that day. Remember, my strap," she said with her eyebrows raised.

The boys looked at each other with surprise and smiled looking at Vaibhav.

Aditi realised they took it another way, so, she rectified herself. "The strap of my sandal." Then she gave a stern look to the boys.

Vaibhav nodded and then turned his face.

Now, this was something that Aditi was not used to. Something she never imagined would happen. A guy just ignored her. However, she didn't find his behaviour rude but different and bizarre in a way.

She couldn't stop herself from thinking about him and reminiscing about his gesture of tying her sandal strap. The moment was imprinted on her mind. But now he is completely ignoring her which confused Aditi about the instant connection she felt between them.

Since then every time she would look at him on campus, he would look in another direction. Many times he changed his path seeing her coming across.

She would always try to be near him during demonstrations, in the laboratory and in the lecture theatre but he always dodged her.

In a few days, everyone knew that the most beautiful and happening girl in the batch was interested in Vaibhav Sinha. And it happens all the time that boys do not try to woo a girl who they think is far beyond what they deserve. So, every other girl was getting the attention of boys and Aditi was busy figuring out what was wrong with him or her that he wouldn't even look at her.

Anyways, since MBBS is one of the toughest courses, everybody remained busy with books most of the time and few of them all the time and Vaibhav was among those few. He was the perfect example of a bookworm. And it turned out that he was the brightest student among his batch.

One day he was just going through the corridor.

"Vaibhav," a sweet voice struck his ears from behind.

He turned back. It was Aditi coming towards him hastily.

"Stop," she panted.

"Don't you dare run away. I have been trying to talk to you for two months and you are avoiding me as if I have a communicable disease," she expressed herself without any hesitation.

"Why do you never look at me?" she complained.

"Because if I look at you more than a second, I won't be able to take my eyes off you. And I don't want that," he said and went away.

Aditi stood there looking at him going. She was completely swayed away by his words, And now, she was even more interested in him.

Boys' Hostel

Prateek (Vaibhav's roommate and friend) – Yaar, everyone knows she likes you. From where do you get the courage to ignore a girl like Aditi Shah? She is the most beautiful girl I've ever seen in person.

Vaibhav didn't even look at Prateek while he said.

Prateek – I am talking to you. Are you not listening?

Vaibhav – The anatomy viva is tomorrow. You better concentrate on that!

Prateek – I will not let you prepare for the viva until you answer my question. What's stopping you from talking to her? Why are you avoiding her?

Vaibhav remained silent for a few minutes as if he was remembering something and then said, "I was completely smitten by her when I saw her for the first time on the stairs. She ran her fingers through her beautiful hair and held the pleats of her shiny mauve-coloured saree with the other hand. She lifted her pleats a little and found that the strap of her sandal was untied. She struggled to do it on her own and I did it for her. I still remember how beautiful those feet were."

Prateek – That means you are also into her. What is the problem then?

Vaibhav – Have you seen her properly?

Prateek – Who hasn't?

Vaibhav – My family's monthly expenses in total might be less than her monthly salon bills. Her father is a diamond merchant and my father is a supervisor in a factory. My mother sold her jewellery to pay my coaching fees when I was preparing for PMT.

I cannot put myself in a position where I would feel ashamed of my family's financial position. Whatever I am today is because of my family. I cannot afford to make them feel so little of themselves by getting involved with a rich girl.

Prateek – You are overthinking it, my friend.

Vaibhav – No, this is called farsightedness.

Prateek – You were born such or become like this in the process.

Vaibhav (interrupting Prateek) – What do you mean?

Prateek – Nothing, Uncle. You keep on studying.

Vaibhav – Yes! I will. At least, I am ahead of her in one field and I would like to keep it so.

A Few Days Later

Vaibhav has noticed that Aditi has now stopped chasing him or trying to talk to him. Now, he was the one stealing glances at her now and then. One day Vaibhav saw that two of their seniors were scolding Aditi and she stood there with her head hung low. He couldn't stop himself from going there and asking what the matter was.

"Oh! You are worried about her," the senior girl taunted.

"That's good. If he is so worried, let's take care of him first," the senior boy said.

"I have a plan. One slap for her or ten slaps for you." the senior girl said to Vaibhav.

Aditi tried to say something but they stopped her from speaking up.

"Let her go," Vaibhav said.

This was the first time he was beaten up by someone in his life. His cheeks turned purple-red.

After the seniors left, Aditi came toward him and before he could turn and go, she said, "You can get beaten up for me but cannot talk to me. I fail to understand this logic of yours."

"Look, we belong to different social strata. We cannot get along," Vaibhav said.

"Oh! What if I was a boy? You wouldn't have thought that way," Aditi said.

"But you are a girl and a very beautiful one and there is a fair chance of me falling in love with you. And I want to avoid that," Vaibhav stated bluntly.

Aditi laughed. She said, "That's insane. I am not asking you to go so far. I believe in living in the moment. You shouldn't let go of what life is offering you by overthinking it. Have you ever wondered why you were there that day to help me with my footwear and not anyone else? It was only you that appeared to rescue me from the wrath of those seniors today. These are signs and I believe in them."

"By the way what have you done? Those seniors were pretty miffed at you," asked Vaibhav.

"Aaah! Don't ask. People get intimidated by me easily. That's my thing. I did nothing. It's their problem."

"They hit you so hard," she winced.

"They did," said Vaibhav, touching his face.

"Friends?" Aditi extended her hand toward him.

He smiled. They shook hands. And went together for the next lecture. Everybody looked at them as they entered the class. Some boys hooted from the back.

Vaibhav turned back and showed his fist to them.

They hooted louder. Aditi laughed at Vaibhav being so uncomfortable with the attention.

"Relax. It's just for now," Aditi pacified him.

The next day, Aditi secured a seat for Vaibhav in the lecture theatre next to her. Vaibhav hesitated a little at first, but then it became their ritual to always secure a seat for each other. They would go to the cafeteria together. Sometimes it was with a group or just the two of them.

"How come you don't like tea?" Vaibhav asked.

"Just like you don't like so many things."

"What are you trying to imply?"

"You say no to everything; club, mall or any sort of outing," Aditi said with a sad face.

"I don't have time for these things. You can go with your other friends. I've no problem," Vaibhav asserted.

"Well. I can but I want you to join me. You are my friend and I don't want you to be upset about me having fun without you," she winked.

He laughed.

"C'mon, it's my birthday next week and we are having a party, I won't listen to any excuse." she asserted.

"Oh! Next week. That I cannot refuse." He replied sipping his tea.

Boys' Hostel

Prateek – You seem lost. What happened?

Vaibhav – Yaar. It's Aditi's birthday next week.

Prateek – Is that a problem?

Vaibhav – No. I wanted to gift her something special but…

Prateek – I get it. No worries, yaar. I'll lend you some money.

Vaibhav – No, I don't want that.

Prateek – Then give her something simple that is in your budget. I am sure she'll like it. Anyway, she knows about your financial situation. By the way, what's going on between you two?

Vaibhav – We are just friends.

Prateek – She friend-zoned you.

Vaibhav – She might have been infatuated with me initially. But now we are just friends.

Prateek – And you? What are your feelings about her?

Vaibhav – I do not deserve her. I knew it in the first place only.

Prateek – Then why are you worried about her birthday gift? Give her anything.

Vaibhav – You won't understand.

Prateek – I tell you one thing, never be a beautiful girl's friend. You will end up crying for her.

Vaibhav – I don't know.

Vaibhav sighed deeply

Prateek – Switch off the lights.

Vaibhav – Hmmm.

Vaibhav pondered over every possibility to give Aditi a nice present.

Next Day At The College

"What's this chaos all about?" Vaibhav asked Priya, Aditi's friend.

Priya – You shouldn't worry as your anatomy file must be complete.

Vaibhav – Yeah…totally.

Soon after, his expression changed, his face lit up, his eyes twinkled with happiness and he got the idea of how he was going to arrange Aditi's birthday gift.

After Three Days In The Lecture Theatre

Lecturer (angrily) – Mr. Vaibhav. You can leave the class if you are drowsy. Can you repeat what we were discussing?

Everybody looked at Vaibhav since he had never failed to answer any question before. He yawned again.

Lecturer – Please leave the lecture theatre right now.

Vaibhav left the class with his head hung low.

The next day also, he looked drowsy. Aditi asked him if he is alright.

"Yeah! Absolutely," Vaibhav answered.

"You can share with me if you have any problem."

"I am fine. Trust me."

"Okay," Aditi nodded.

Two days before Aditi's birthday party, Vaibhav asked Priya to help him to find a gift for Aditi. She happily agreed and they went shopping.

At The Mall

"So, let's start the hunt for the perfect gift." He was excited and nervous both at the same time.

"She is fond of perfumes and bags," Priya suggested looking at Vaibhav.

"Aditi is so lucky to have you in her life," Priya said while looking for a gift.

He looked at Priya with suspicion.

"Oh, c'mon! I know that you prepared the anatomy files of other students while being up all night," Priya exclaimed.

"How come you know this?" Vaibhav asked, startled.

"Prateek told me."

"Do you guys talk to each other?"

"Forget that. Let's focus on getting what we came for," Priya made an excuse.

"I will not spare him. Idiot!" Vaibhav murmured.

Priya gazed at him from the corner of her eye and chuckled listening to him.

They got a nice handbag for Aditi from a high-end brand.

At The Birthday Party

Aditi was looking fabulous in a shimmery black outfit. The party was speaking for itself of its splendour.

"Where were you?" Aditi shouted at Vaibhav as he entered.

He was an introvert and felt quite out of the place but managed to mask his real feelings.

Everyone cheered as Aditi cut the cake and she took the first piece of cake to feed Vaibhav and everyone cheered louder.

"Here is your gift. Happy birthday once again," Vaibhav extended the gift to her.

"Thanks! And by the way, it was not needed."

"I hope you may like it," Vaibhav smiled.

"No doubt," Aditi asserted.

She dragged him to the dance floor. Vaibhav resisted initially but gave up eventually and joined her. The music was so loud that Vaibhav couldn't hear his phone ringing. After an hour or maybe more when he checked his phone, there were 10 missed calls from his elder sister. There was a message too and after reading that Vaibhav's face became pale and his pulse dropped. He looked flustered and headed outside into the lobby. Aditi saw him going outside and followed him.

Chapter – 2

Vaibhav was in the lobby on the phone pacing anxiously.

"You look miserable. What happened?" Aditi asked him after he was done talking on the phone.

"My father had a heart attack. He is in the ICU and I have no clue what to do. My family needs me right now," Vaibhav replied as he threw his hands up in the air and sighed deeply.

He had spent all he had on Aditi's gift. He couldn't even get a train ticket as he was completely out of money.

Before he could say or think anything Aditi said, "Let's go to the hostel and change first before going to the airport."

"Airport?" Vaibhav looked at her surprisingly.

"Let's go. We can talk on our way to the hostel," Aditi held his hand and they left the party in the middle.

They reached the airport just in time and took a flight from New Delhi to Lucknow and a cab thereafter to his hometown.

"Thanks for all this. I shall repay you as soon as possible," Vaibhav said to her.

"Shut up. Anything for the family."

He smiled gingerly.

At The Hospital

"Bhaiya!" Vaibhav's younger sister shouted seeing him.

He went up to his mother, touched her feet, hugged her and asked about his father's condition. His mother was not aware of the condition of his father at all. She looked anxious and despondent.

Aditi and Vaibhav talked to the concerned staff about Vaibhav's father's situation. They were taken seriously at the hospital as they were students of the most elite medical college in the nation. They got to know that his father is out of danger now but was still under observation.

Vaibhav introduced Aditi to his family and asked his sisters to take care of her. He had asked Aditi and his family to go home as he wanted to stay at the hospital with his father. Aditi refused to go and insisted to stay with him only. His sisters and mother went home to get some rest as they had a tough time handling the emergency.

"Are you okay?" Aditi asked Vaibhav.

"Hmm," he nodded.

"Aren't you tired?" Vaibhav asked her.

"Little bit. But it is okay! I can manage,"

"Thanks," Vaibhav said while looking at the floor.

"How many times are you going to thank me? You would have done the same for my family. Wouldn't you?"

He looked at her and nodded. She held his hand and they spent the night at the hospital to attend to any unforeseen situations.

Early Morning Next Day

Vaibhav's elder sister came to the hospital. She looked for them and smiled at the way they were sleeping. Vaibhav was sleeping with his neck extended back and mouth open. Aditi was sleeping with her head on his arm, her mouth open and a bit of saliva dripping from her mouth and soaking his shirt a little.

Vaibhav's sister tapped his shoulder.

He was startled to see his sister and took a few seconds to come back to his senses.

Very lightly he drew his arm and stretched it to get relief from muscle spasms.

Aditi was still sleeping. Vaibhav was already embarrassed to see his sister and now he hesitated to wake Aditi up.

"You two look very tired. I will be here. You should go home, freshen up and have breakfast," his sister Shilpa said.

"Aditi. Hey! Get up." Vaibhav tried to wake her up.

She rose with puffy eyes, looked around with half-opened eyes, slumped and fell asleep again. Vaibhav's sister chuckled seeing her. Vaibhav lifted Aditi. He grabbed her shoulders and patted her cheek.

"Wake up," he said, rolling his eyes.

"Hmm. Is it morning already?" Aditi asked, rubbing her eyes.

Vaibhav blinked his eyes in response. Aditi straightened her back, tried to look as awake as possible and greeted Shilpa (Vaibhav's sister).

Vaibhav and Aditi went home while his sister remained at the hospital.

While they were having breakfast, Vaibhav's younger sister whispered in his ear, "Is everyone in Delhi beautiful like her? She looks even more beautiful than actresses."

Vaibhav smiled and said, "No."

"Mom, we have to catch a flight from Lucknow. We haven't applied for any leaves in college. Everything here seems pretty fine. Papa will come home by evening. I've already talked to the staff there," Vaibhav said to his mother.

"Yes. You both should leave. Your studies shouldn't be hampered at any cost," his mother replied.

On Their Way Back

"Your sisters are cute," Aditi said to Vaibhav.

"Hmm."

"What happened?" Aditi asked.

"We left your birthday party in haste. What would everybody be thinking?" Vaibhav expressed his concern.

"Don't worry. I've told Priya. She will have us covered."

"Girls can think and do so many things at the same time," Vaibhav applauded.

Aditi shrugged her shoulders and smiled.

At The College

Aditi was busy putting all her birthday gifts in her almirahs and she stopped seeing Vaibhav's gift. Unlike all other gifts, she opened this one.

"Wow! I am impressed. He has got good taste," Aditi said excitingly.

"Yes," Priya said in a deep voice.

"What?" Aditi was suspicious of Priya and sensed that she was hiding something.

"Nothing," Priya replied

"There is something. I can read your face. What's wrong?" Aditi insisted.

"Yaar. I was touched when I came to know that he worked so hard to give you this. You might have many such bags but this one is special," said Priya.

"I didn't follow you," Aditi frowned.

"He prepared anatomy files of other students for 5 consecutive nights just to be able to give you this gift. Prateek told the students that he knows someone who can get work done in exchange for money. It was Vaibhav because he wanted to give you something in accord with your standard. He is a gem," Priya told her.

Aditi's eyes got welled up. She said nothing and was touched deeply knowing about it.

"Promise me you will never let him know about you knowing this," Priya requested Aditi.

"Hmm," Aditi replied.

"Good night," Priya went to sleep.

Next Day At College

"How is uncle?" Aditi asked Vaibhav.

"He is fine. I've talked to him," Vaibhav replied.

Past events amplified the bond they shared. Vaibhav was completely swayed away by her down-to-earth attitude, and how she helped him with the recent critical emergency at his home. Aditi was deeply touched by Vaibhav's efforts to give her a present on her birthday.

"Oh! I must tell you. I loved the bag you gave me. It's so classy. I like your choice," Aditi said.

"You are being modest. You must be having better stuff than that one."

"You are an idiot," Aditi smirked.

"Maybe. Anyway, leave all that behind. We have exams approaching and we should focus on our studies," Vaibhav said in a serious tone.

"Yeah! I am damn nervous. You have to help me," Aditi said, making a baby face.

"I don't believe in a group study but we can try."

Boys' Hostel

"What happened, old man? Why do you look so serious?" Prateek asked Vaibhav.

"Aditi wanted to have group study but I am not comfortable with it. How do I say no to her?" Vaibhav looked confused.

"Please, you should agree to it. At least, this way I will get to be with Priya." Prateek said with enthusiasm.

"What's cooking?" Vaibhav asked notoriously.

"I like her," Prateek smiled.

"Aah!" Vaibhav teased him.

"I am not like you. I like her, I know that and I am going to tell her that one day, soon."

"Why didn't you tell me about it earlier?" Vaibhav kicked Prateek.

They hit each other playfully.

Next Day At The Cafeteria

All four of them were sitting together when Prateek proposed the idea, "My brother's flat is well furnished and it's not far from here. We can go for a group study there."

"Nice," Aditi exclaimed.

Priya and Vaibhav didn't say anything but didn't deny also.

It always happens among a group of friends. Some are super active and fun-loving while others are always silent. Prateek and Aditi planned everything: permission, food, and other arrangements. Vaibhav and Priya just followed them. Prateek was the most excited among the four of them and barely thought of exams once. He was exulted over the thought of spending time with Priya.

At Prateek's Brother's Flat

It was a nice, spacious and airy 3 BHK flat with a house help for maintenance. All four of them settled quickly and gathered in the hall to discuss the strategy for exam preparation. Since Vaibhav was the smartest of all, rest three of them followed the strategy that he had planned. Vaibhav had already mentioned he might walk out any minute he found that this setup isn't working for him. But fortunately, it was a comfortable, cosy and nice place to concentrate and give your 100 percent.

Around midnight, Priya asked, "Who wants tea?"

"I never say no to tea," Vaibhav replied.

As Priya stood up and went into the kitchen, Prateek instantly followed her saying, "Let me help her find things in the kitchen."

Aditi smiled and said to Vaibhav, "Your friend is up to something."

"You'll get to know eventually. Now, do not distract me," Vaibhav said bluntly.

"Okay! Grumpy grandpa," Aditi smirked.

"It's been twenty minutes. What are they doing in the kitchen?" Vaibhav asked while making a curious face.

"I am not allowed to talk," Aditi said, raising her eyebrows.

"Oh, c'mon." Vaibhav winced.

Prateek and Priya came out of the kitchen.

"We have made sandwiches too," Priya said.

"Great! You two are getting along well and these sandwiches are looking great," Aditi stated.

Midnight snacks and friends are a great combination. After this little break, they got back to their books. After an hour, Aditi fell asleep on the couch only and the rest three of them went to their respective rooms. This little arrangement for group study sparked something between Priya and Prateek. Vaibhav checked on Aditi twice during the night as she was sleeping on the couch in the hall.

Next Day At The Cafeteria

"My neck is strained. It's so painful. You didn't care at all. I was sleeping on the sofa uncomfortably and got muscle spasms," Aditi complained.

"What did you expect me to do?" Vaibhav asked curiously.

"You should have lifted me and made me sleep in the room."

"Like a Hindi film hero!" Vaibhav laughed.

"You are nowhere near to it," Aditi winced.

"I know I am not. Okay, I am sorry. I'll not let you sleep on the sofa from now on. Can I have my tea now?" Vaibhav pacified.

She was still miffed and babbled about her neck.

Prateek and Priya were busy in their world. They were talking to each other so seriously as if no one else was there.

"Look at them! Your friend is a straight shooter. He won't take much time," Aditi said while looking at Prateek and Priya.

"He is your friend too and he is a nice guy," Vaibhav replied.

"They look cute together. Don't they?" Aditi smiled as she asked Vaibhav.

"No idea," Vaibhav frowned.

"Were you born like this or became like this over time?" Aditi said.

"Like what?" Vaibhav asked raising his eyebrows.

"Cold and impassive," Aditi exclaimed.

Vaibhav looked clueless. Why was Aditi giving such adjectives to him? He concentrated on having his tea.

At The Flat

"Let's order pizza before starting with the preparation," Aditi said.

Prateek and Priya reacted positively.

"It seems you all are on a picnic," Vaibhav taunted.

"You should shut your mouth, Grumpy grandpa!" Aditi teased him.

Everyone laughed.

All three of them pounced on the pizza box as soon as it arrived.

"Mine has no mushrooms on it," Aditi pretended to cry.

Vaibhav gave all the mushrooms he had on his pizza.

"Don't you like mushrooms?" asked Aditi.

"It doesn't matter. If you want them, you should have them," Vaibhav replied.

Vaibhav always used to say these small things with massive hidden feelings behind them without even looking at Aditi. And she was always left spellbound.

"And what does that mean?" she asked this time.

"That you should get everything you wish for. At least I wish that," Vaibhav said.

Aditi watched him longingly and then concentrated on her pizza and of course mushrooms over it.

They cleared their doubts among themselves and helped each other with the preparation. It was 11:30 pm when Aditi went into the kitchen and came back with three cups of tea.

"Oh wow! You made tea for us without us telling you to do so?" Priya said happily.

"Yeah! Because some people are reluctant to express what they want," Aditi said, staring at Vaibhav.

Vaibhav smiled gingerly and everybody continued with what they were doing.

The Night Before The First Exam

Aditi's face was all sweaty. It appeared as if she was going to have a panic attack. Vaibhav looked at her and asked, "What happened, Aditi? And where is Priya?"

"She is with Prateek. I am so anxious. I feel like I forgot everything and I won't be able to write anything for the exam tomorrow." Aditi replied frenetically.

Vaibhav made her sit, gave her a glass of water, held her hands and said, "Listen, you know everything and you will be able to write it. Do not worry at all. Just stop overthinking about it and try to remain calm. Come, let's tuck you to bed. Try to catch some sleep."

"Sit here for a while and you can go once I am asleep," Aditi requested.

"Don't worry! I am here." Vaibhav sat by her side holding her hand.

Aditi had this magical power to sleep anywhere within minutes. It took her twenty minutes to fall asleep. Vaibhav drew his hand slowly, he looked at her longingly.

Priya ran into him while he was coming out of the room. She was surprised to see him coming out of her room.

"It's nothing. She was having a nervous breakdown. It's all okay now, she is sleeping." Vaibhav stuttered.

"Oh my God! I am sorry I was not there for her but thanks for taking care of her." Priya showed gratitude.

"That's okay! How are things going with Prateek?" Vaibhav asked her to change the topic.

"Pretty well. Let these exams get over first. I am too scared."

"Don't be scared. We are good. We prepared well. Good night and best of luck for tomorrow," Vaibhav walked towards his room.

Next Day After The Exam

"So, how was your exam?" Vaibhav asked Aditi as she was very nervous the day before.

"I think I did pretty okay," Aditi wanted assurance from Vaibhav.

"Good," Vaibhav said in a comforting way.

"How about you?"

"Average,"

"His average is our awesome," Prateek laughed.

"I need to prepare for the next exam alone," Priya said in a gloomy tone.

"Why? What happened?" Prateek asked, worried.

"I think I am not going to get even passing marks," Priya was just about to cry.

"I am going to the hostel. I need to be alone," Priya turned around and started crying.

"Priya…listen… I won't bother you. Please don't cry."

Priya didn't care to listen to him. It was Vaibhav who convinced her to come along for group study because he knew she was not in the right frame of mind to cope with the situation alone.

At The Flat

"How can she blame me? I fail to understand." Prateek was feeling disgusted about Priya's behaviour.

"Girls are emotionally fragile," Vaibhav tried to make a point on her behalf.

"This is a major 'turn-off' for me. I cannot handle such situations, as you did today. I do not want to be with a girl like this," Prateek said in frustration.

"It's too soon to say anything. Maybe her exam went effing bad. She could fail and it was just an outburst. You guys get along so well. Don't get disheartened." Vaibhav made him understand.

"I am trapped. She is not talking to me and I am already missing her. What is happening?" Prateek said with a poker face. Vaibhav laughed and asked him to focus on the exam first and leave everything else to fall into its place on its own.

As Aditi took care of Priya and calmed her, Priya felt sorry for not being there for her when Aditi was having a nervous breakdown. She was only saying this to Aditi and they were having their moment of friendship and sisterly affection, suddenly out of nowhere Priya said. "I want to see him," as today Prateek was studying in his room instead of the hall unlike always.

Vaibhav and Aditi looked at each other and then towards Priya and bowed in front of her saying, "You are great ma'am."

Priya looked restless and said "Whatever". She stood up and went straight to Prateek's room.

"Should we follow her?" Aditi asked with a strange look on her face.

"No! leave them alone." Vaibhav took a deep breath.

"I cannot do it," Priya said to Prateek as she entered the room.

"Me either," Prateek stood up.

"Feeling so relieved, talking to you."

"I was going to say something like that only, I was missing you."

They came out of the room hand in hand and looked fine.

"This was the lamest fight I had ever seen. I will deal with you guys after exams," Aditi squinted her eyes while saying so.

All four of them laughed and instantly got themselves busy with the books.

The first year of their medical degree was an amalgamation of nervousness, sadness, anxiety, fear, happiness, and euphoria. And now it was time to go home as the festival of Holi was approaching and so were the holidays.

Chapter – 3

The happiest place on earth is your college hostel if you are friends with the right kind of people. The same was the case with our Aditi, Vaibhav, Priya and Prateek.

Friends are like family members which we choose for ourselves. We can share our unfiltered thoughts with them, they take care of us like parents and we have fun with them as we have with siblings and share happiness and sorrows. They are there for us during our highs and lows in life, every hardship, every setback and every achievement. They bring us back to the track of life if we ever derail. A good friend is like that big tree you can take shelter during a storm.

"Let's join the class for the party before everyone leaves for their home," said Aditi.

"Yaar. I am not so much into parties. I can be with you guys only. I cannot bear the whole class altogether," Vaibhav gave an excuse.

Aditi looked at him with sheer discontentment.

"I know, I am grumpy. Whatever you say, I am not coming. But you guys can go. Don't miss a chance to enjoy yourself just because your friend is so boring." Vaibhav tried to explain.

"Common, let's push him from the fifth floor. He is such a loser," Prateek said.

"I have an awesome idea," Aditi jumped with excitement.

"I am all ears. Bring it on," Prateek showed interest.

"Let's go to Rishikesh together, before going home. We'll do river rafting and camping. It will be a lifetime experience. What do you think?" Aditi asked with enthusiasm and a sparkle in her eyes.

"I am all in. Solid plan," Prateek confirmed.

"Me too," Priya asserted.

Three of them looked at Vaibhav together with evil smiles.

"I don't think you all need me to say anything. I have no choice," Vaibhav smiled.

"We are going!" Aditi shouted out of excitement and hugged Vaibhav suddenly, causing him to lose balance.

As always Aditi and Prateek planned everything, Vaibhav and Priya just followed and were ready to enjoy the fruit of Aditi and Prateek's hard work.

On Their Way To Rishikesh

Vaibhav – I am glad we are doing this.

Aditi – Really! So, you have started taking life with light feet. You know, sometimes I wonder about how Vaibhav would look laughing out loud or shouting out of excitement or driving rashly or doing other crazy stuff that boys are into. Unleash yourself of all the restraints. Life is beautiful. Enjoy it.

Vaibhav (after taking a deep breath) – When I was 7 or 8 years old, I got very good marks. I think I was in the third standard. I was eagerly waiting for my father to show him my report card. He came, he saw it and said: "This is not enough. You should improve." All my excitement vanished at that very moment.

After that incident, I started to play less and study more. Fortunately, I got better marks but again he said I should improve.

He used to tell all my relatives that I study 12 hours a day, which I was not. It created pressure upon me that I should study 12 hours a day.

I never participated in any of the functions at school. I never went to my relatives' weddings or celebrations and nearly stopped playing also.

Boys of my age used to play cricket, football and all sorts of games but I remained busy achieving the target my father had set for me. He would proudly brag in front of his friends and relatives that I do nothing other than study, no movies, no sports or adventures.

Even when I felt like watching a movie with the boys or chilling with them, it always occurred to me what my father would think then. So, I always restricted myself from doing things that I wanted to do otherwise.

Eventually, I turned myself into a person who would never have a hankering to do anything other than study.

I lived a life with no colours at all. Now also when I go home, no one asks me how I am, how I am feeling or what I want. Everyone just asks about academics. All they talk about is my sister's dowry and how I can help with that, my family's financial problems, my father's plans to do this and that, when I'll start earning, etc.

No one ever bothered to ask about my feelings. I have missed so much in life and I'm probably never going to relive it. My elder sister is the only person with whom I share my feelings and discuss things that I don't share even with my mother.

But you know, it's not their fault. When you have to think twice before getting a new shirt for yourself or when you have to manage other things to save money, to buy a ticket to visit your son. Who cares about feelings?

Life is complicated. No one is right and no one is completely wrong. It's just a matter of perspective and situation.

Aditi looked at his face while he was looking out of the window. She felt sorry for bringing it up, about restraints and taking life lightly.

She held his hand and they said nothing to each other but still, Vaibhav could feel the compassion.

When they got off the bus, Vaibhav said, "I cannot feel my shoulder. If there was an award for sleeping anywhere anytime, you will be the undisputed winner."

Aditi shrugged her shoulders and looked around.

"It's not that dark yet, let's hire scooters and explore the place," Vaibhav suggested.

"Literally! Grumpy grandpa is saying that. I can't believe my ears," Aditi was astounded hearing it from him.

All four of them had a wonderful time roaming around the city, clicking pictures and having food.

Aditi insisted on riding the scooter and Vaibhav eventually agreed after denying it, at first. She never rode a two-wheeler before this.

"I am scared, be careful," Vaibhav insinuated.

"Don't worry," Aditi was thrilled with her tiny adventure.

"Be careful. Look straight," Vaibhav kept on saying repeatedly and yet they fell off and got bruised themselves badly.

"Are you alright?" Vaibhav asked.

"I am sorry," Aditi said, making a baby face.

"Leave it! Are you okay? Come, there is a medical store. Let's get first aid," Vaibhav said pointing towards a medical store. Prateek and Priya also reached there when Vaibhav was cleaning Aditi's wound at her elbow. Aditi noticed that Vaibhav ignored that he also got hurt and she pointed out looking at his trouser which was torn off at the knee and got wet with blood. Prateek and Priya helped both of them and after they were done bandaging the wounds. Vaibhav narrated how they fell and all of them laughed hard for a few minutes.

At The Camping Site On The Banks Of The River Ganga

"Wow! I'll be in a camp for the first time in my life," exclaimed Priya.

"The aura of this place is just amazing," Aditi looked around, delighted.

"Priya and I will be in the same camp. Right?" Prateek asked notoriously.

"How did you reach this conclusion?" Priya said harshly.

"Why not?" Prateek asked, pretending to be naïve.

Vaibhav stood there smiling and Aditi teased Priya, "C'mon. Tell us. Why not?"

Priya gave a stern look to Aditi.

Anyways after having dinner they went to their respective camps because the next day they were supposed to go river rafting early morning.

At midnight, when Aditi woke up to drink water, Priya was not there in the camp. She peeped outside the camp and was surprised to see Vaibhav sitting on the ground near the water. It was cold out there, she took her blanket and ambled up to him.

The night was moonlit and a bit cold. Amidst all this, the sound of water was further enchanting.

"Aren't you feeling cold?" Aditi said, extending the blanket towards him.

"Little bit," he replied.

"Giving privacy to your friend. You could have come in mine; how long do you plan to sit here?" Aditi threw questions.

"I am imbibing the aura of this place within me," he replied, looking at the sky full of stars.

"My life is like this water, destined to reach a certain destination, taking a pre-decided path."

"I am glad you opened up to me on our way here," Aditi said affectionately.

"Before this, I never felt like sharing with anybody."

"I am privileged," Aditi said, looking at the sky.

"Your childhood must be so different than mine, wasn't it?" Vaibhav asked.

"Different in a certain way and same in a certain way."

"When I was a kid in school, every other girl envied me. I never had a friend who would understand me, the inner me and what I am from within.

While growing up I was paid extra attention by the teachers. However, I was good at academics but my classmates would say, it's all about good looks.

When I was in the tenth standard, I had a boyfriend. He always used to brag about me in front of his friends and I never liked it.

I was a very pampered kid. My family loved me so much. I belong to a business family, as you know, all they talk about is money, business, growth and showing off. They always say that I will get married to a family with a bigger business house than us."

Vaibhav sighed deeply.

"They say that not me, I could have done MBA and got married to a rich guy and settled abroad. But, I would have lost myself in that big fat wedding, tons of jewellery, fake smiles and ending up with a person who would treat me as an asset. I would only need to look beautiful, shop for things, throw parties and that's it.

It wouldn't be my achievement. So, I opted to prepare for something which was not easy and getting through it gave me a sense of achievement and self-pride. I wanted to prove to myself and everyone else that I am not just another rich beautiful Gujarati girl who wanted to settle abroad and have a luxurious life. I am someone who has a mind and soul and wants to explore the possibilities of life and want to end up with someone who will bring peace to me, touch my soul, far beyond the bodily dimensions and attraction."

She leaned towards him and rested her head on his shoulder. He put his arm across her shoulder and tilted his head towards her.

Striping away their souls to each other under the stars, on the bank of the holy Ganga, was no less than a magical experience for them.

They sat there in one blanket, talking to each other until sunrise. The sound of rumbling water was no less than soulful classical music. On one side the moon was hiding behind the clouds and on the other side, the sun was all set to rise, turning the sky into a colourful painting…saffron with hints of red and pink.

The view was deliriously beautiful and enchanting. They looked at the sunrise hand in hand as if the sun and moon were witnesses of their souls getting united.

"You should take some rest now. We have to go rafting today," Vaibhav said to Aditi.

"Your shoulder?" Aditi asked with a smile.

"More than fine," Vaibhav smiled.

And they went back to their tents.

Before River Rafting

Priya was so nervous to try it as she had a fear of water bodies.

"Stop fooling us. You always do things that you deny doing at first," Aditi joked.

Priya blushed and hit Aditi with her bag childishly.

While the girls were getting all geared up with the life jacket and the headgear and all that stuff, Prateek asked Vaibhav, "What do you seem so happy about?"

"It's far beyond your understanding, buddy. But yeah, I am happy," Vaibhav asserted.

"You are intense, man. I would have a crush on you if I was a girl," Prateek clung upon Vaibhav.

"And I would have rejected you outright," Vaibhav smirked.

Prateek bombarded him with 4 or 5 abusive words and they both laughed and all of them went rafting. They had a lifetime experience. Priya was scared at first but enjoyed it once they started doing it. Rafting, I mean.

After having lunch, they booked a cab to New Delhi and after dropping Prateek and Priya at the railway station, Aditi and Vaibhav went to the airport. Aditi had a flight to Ahmedabad and Vaibhav went along to see her off.

"Now since there is no train to Lucknow, you have to go by bus. You shouldn't have missed your train," Aditi said with her big ocean-like eyes looking affectionately at Vaibhav.

"I do not have any answer to your question. But I know you wanted me to come with you to see you off. Isn't it?" Vaibhav asked her.

Aditi smiled and said, "Smart! Question for a question."

"I think you should go inside now and…Happy Holi," Vaibhav didn't look at her face this time.

"Yeah!" She waved and turned to go inside.

Chapter – 4

At Vaibhav's Home

"How come you are late? You were supposed to come two days before," Vaibhav's father asked him, quite miffed.

"I went to Rishikesh with friends,"

"What for?" Father asked squinting his eyes.

"I wanted to. That's why," Vaibhav said looking at the floor.

"Here, day in and day out we are under stress managing Shilpa's dowry. And you are busy enjoying your vacation." His father was visibly disappointed.

"I can never make you happy. Whatever I do, you have a problem with it. I didn't spend a single penny, my friends arranged everything, I didn't like it but I had no choice. I am not blaming anyone. I know we are going through a rough phase, but I do not want to be shamed for giving two days of my life to my friends. It's not a big deal." Vaibhav stormed out of the room.

He was feeling bad for the outburst he had in front of his father for the first time in his life. On the other hand, Vaibhav's father was surprised and felt quite low seeing his son being so harsh upon him.

Vaibhav wondered if everything is the same, then what made him say such harsh words to his father. Perhaps, he had feelings for Aditi now and he was scared of making Aditi face the reality of the world that he belonged to. Albeit, he had told her many times about the financial status of his family, still, how could she cope with the mindset of his family? She knew nothing about the problems of a middle-class family, the mindset and the authoritarian attitude of the head of the family who has problems with every damn thing involving expenditure.

Vaibhav felt trapped in mixed emotions. On one hand, he wanted to take his relationship a notch up with Aditi as he acknowledged the mutual admiration, comfort and understanding between them. On the other hand, he didn't want to drag her into the unfavourable situations he had at his home. There was a great deal of consternation growing within him and getting amplified every passing minute.

Vaibhav regretted speaking his mind out in front of his father and breaking the glass ceiling for him... that his son only does whatever he is asked to do.

He pitied himself because he could not express his love to the girl he was madly in love with due to the situation.

After hours of contemplation, he came back home and apologised to his father. His father didn't utter a single word.

At night, Vaibhav's elder sister, Shilpa, came up to him and asked if she could give him a head massage.

"Sure! I need that," Vaibhav complied.

"You okay?" Shilpa asked.

"Kind of."

"I know why you are frustrated."

"You do?" Vaibhav's eyes showed interest in the forthcoming conversation.

"You are worried and anxious because you love her and you don't want her to be a part of the mess that you are a part of."

"How do you always know about the things going in my head? But this is my family. Please don't address it as a mess. It's just that… I do not want to be questioned every time I do something for my happiness. Being a family we all should have a sort of understanding and should be considerate of each other.

I am feeling very bad for talking to him this way. I hope he has forgiven me," Vaibhav delved into his thoughts again.

"Look! You are worrying too much. You are overthinking it. In a few years, you will be a very efficient and successful doctor. I might be married by then and once our father's financial responsibilities will be shared by you or taken over by you, he will get relaxed. He is like this because he has small earnings and he is having a hard time managing things. You are in one of the nation's most elite institutions. You don't need our family's fortune to lead a good life. You have a bright future. Always keep that in mind." Shilpa confronted him.

"Thanks, Didi," Vaibhav showed gratitude.

"My privilege," Shilpa hugged him.

His sister's words calmed the storm rising within him.

At Aditi's Home

"You will be the first doctor in our family. We are so proud of you," Aditi's mother expressed her happiness.

"Thanks, Mom."

"What's your plan? Will you get married to a doctor?" mother asked curiously.

"Don't you have any other topic, Mom? It will be my second year now. I have to complete college then I have to do my post-graduation. Who cares about marriage?" Aditi said, irritated.

"Okay! I won't talk about marriage. Don't get angry. Many proposals are coming in for you but we ignored them by saying that our daughter is in medical college and that she will marry a doctor only." Her mother explained.

"Good," Aditi asserted.

"Is there anything you want to tell me? It looks like you have to vent out something." Her mom curiously asked her.

"How do you always know about everything?" Aditi said surprisingly.

"I am your mother. You will know about your kids when you have them. It's natural." Her mother boasted.

"His name is Vaibhav. He is so simple, kind, intelligent and compassionate. I like him." Aditi told her mother sheepishly.

"Oh! Tell me more." Aditi's mother showed interest.

"I've never seen a guy like him before. It was a very sweet encounter when I met him the first time." Aditi narrated in detail how they became friends.

The mother interrupted her in the middle of her narration. "How does he look?"

"He is very tall, slim and has a wheatish complexion. He is charming. Looks don't count that much for me.

He is so caring and not just towards me but for other friends too."

"What does his father do? I mean what kind of family does he belong to?" Mother asked in a serious tone.

"His father works as a supervisor in a factory. His mother is a homemaker. He has two sisters who must be doing graduation or something like that. I am not sure." Aditi replied.

"Are you serious about him? Seeing his financial status, I can assure you that your father won't be allowing you to marry him." Her mother was firm yet gentle.

"C'mon, Mom! First of all, as of now, we have not even defined our relationship and he is the brightest student in our batch. He has a super bright future, who cares about what his father does? By the way, don't discuss what I've told you with anybody."

"Hmm." Aditi's mother walked away quietly.

Festivals play an important role in Indian society. For the underprivileged, it's the time to get new things and eat without rationing and for the privileged, it's the only time when all the family members spend time with each other otherwise everyone remains busy in their world.

Priya and Prateek remained busy talking to each other on phone during their stay at their respective homes.

This Holi was different for each of them, unlike every other year.

This time every visitor who came to Aditi's home praised her hard work for getting into an institution like AIIMS. She was glad to see respect for her in their eyes for something she had achieved on her own.

Vaibhav again apologised to his father and his father also expressed his affection towards him which was a rare thing for him to do.

Chapter – 5

Everybody was back in Delhi and it was time for their first-year exam results.

As everyone has anticipated, Vaibhav Sinha topped the first year's professional exams. Aditi managed to secure good marks, Prateek got average marks but Priya couldn't get through in one of the subjects, the one after which she panicked during the exams. Her friends showed their support which helped her to remain quite stable and composed. Prateek was afraid that Priya's shortcomings would affect his relationship with her. But nothing of that sort happened.

Vaibhav was behaving a little differently from how he behaved before going home. Aditi asked him several times but every time he evaded a reasonable explanation for his altered behaviour.

Aditi speculated that something must have had happened at his home. Upon insisting so much he told her that he is not in the right frame of mind to discuss anything and just wanted to concentrate on his studies.

Aditi decided to support him with whatever he has decided for them and they continued to be friends only masking their feelings for each other.

By the middle of the second year when there were couples all around: serious ones, symbiotic ones, purely physical ones and then there were Vaibhav and Aditi who got famous at first as a cool couple. But now speculations were running rife that they were just goofing around. This orchestrated the feeling in some boys that now they had a chance to woo Aditi Shah, the diamond of the batch, as some would say. And at the same time feelings of some girls also surfaced for the topper of the class. But when both of them didn't pay any attention to petty incidents, everything was back to normal. The two of them were left alone and were now considered unattainable.

Their friendship grew stronger day by day, the comfort between them was inexplicable. They both were there for each other for everything. Since Vaibhav never talked about defining their relationship, Aditi also left that stone unturned and was going by the flow. Priya and Prateek were in a serious relationship. Their families had known about them and everything was as smooth as butter.

One day after the four of them were back after a day out, Aditi seemed so dull.

Priya asked her, "What happened to you?"

"Nothing," Aditi replied.

"Don't be a drama queen. Just tell me," Priya insisted.

"First promise me, you will not judge me," Aditi asked.

"Okay, I won't. Now tell me."

"I envy you sometimes. Looking at you two having a mushy kind of relationship, feeling of being in love and certainty…that he is the one, I want that too. It seems that we have been in a friend zone for ages and Vaibhav is not making any effort to take a step forward in our relationship. My relationship with him is stagnant. I want more but how do I make him understand this? I like him so much and we share an amazing bond. But it's not enough for me. I hope you are getting my point," Aditi poured her heart out.

"I do," Priya nodded.

"Maybe you should give him the impression that you are interested in dating other people and he will get jealous and will try to move forward in the relationship," Priya suggested.

"I do not want to hurt him and he is not like other guys. He might think that I got bored of him and he might leave me seriously to date other guys. I can't take this risk. He is so sensitive," Aditi countered.

"Then wait until he realises that your relationship is in a dormant state and you guys need to stir up things," Priya said.

"Hmmm. Let's see. But I am happy for you and Prateek," Aditi said with a smile on her face.

"Thanks! Touchwood." Priya replied.

Before Aditi got asleep she gave a second thought to what Priya had said to her regarding making Vaibhav jealous.

With friendships, love affairs, practical exams, vivas, exams, projects and sweet and sour experiences the second year was over and yet again Vaibhav turned out to be the highest scorer.

One day all four of them were sitting together in the cafeteria having coffee when some classmates came up to them. One guy among them said, "Listen. You guys have to join us for the party tonight. After all, we are friends, right?"

"You know I am not a party person. So, count me out. I can only speak for myself. These three can join you for the party," Vaibhav replied to them.

"What about you, Aditi? Some seniors are also coming." Those boys asked Aditi.

"Yeah! Why not? All of us will come," Aditi replied.

After those guys left, they had a brief discussion.

"Are we seriously going?" Prateek asked.

"Only if Vaibhav is coming along," Aditi replied.

"See, I feel guilty when you guys don't go anywhere just because of me. Why should you guys be spared from having fun because of me? You all should go if you want to," Vaibhav insisted.

"If you feel guilty, why don't you come along?" Aditi countered.

"Because I feel uncomfortable among them. I don't want to explain to anyone why I don't like parties. I just don't." Vaibhav was quite pissed off.

"You throw more tantrums than girls," Aditi was pretty annoyed with Vaibhav's conduct.

"Whatever!" Vaibhav stood up and walked back to his class while leaving the three of them there.

Prateek said, "He seems upset."

He was worried for Vaibhav.

At The Hostel

Vaibhav was talking over the phone when Prateek entered the room.

"Please go ahead. Sell the land. I don't want anything. If it's for Didi, I am totally in favour of it." He hung up when he noticed Prateek was there.

Prateek – Everything alright at home?

Vaibhav – Yeah!

Prateek – You can tell me.

Vaibhav (shouted) – What will you do if I tell you? Why does everyone want to know everything? My father is selling our ancestral property for my sister's dowry. Now you know.

Prateek – It's okay, bro. I was trying to be supportive. I am sorry, I won't ask again.

The next minute, Vaibhav realised he was rude to Prateek for no reason and so, he apologised.

Prateek – We are brothers, man. No need to say sorry. Let's chill today. I will lift your mood. Let the girls go to the party alone.

Vaibhav – No, you should go along.

Prateek – No! I want to be with you.

Vaibhav – Alright!

Prateek took him to his engineering friends and all of them enticed him to smoke weed. Vaibhav got so high that he had no idea where his phone was.

At The Party

Aditi dressed to kill and both the girls arrived at the party without boys. Aditi was enjoying herself ignoring the fact that one of the seniors was hitting on her and he only asked those boys to go and invite the group to the party so that she would come with or without Vaibhav. It was almost midnight. Both of them tried to reach out to Vaibhav and Prateek but neither of them picked up the call. Eventually, the girls had to take favour from that senior and his friend to drop them at the hostel.

Aditi was so mad at Vaibhav that she decided to date other guys just to make him realise her worth. The next day both Vaibhav and Prateek didn't turn up for the classes. Aditi and Priya were angry and worried at the same time. Luckily Prateek received Priya's call during lunch hours and told her that they are alright. Aditi was still pissed at Vaibhav.

It was announced in the class that clinical postings will be assigned to the students from now. Aditi and Vaibhav got posted in different departments but Prateek and Priya got posted in the same department.

It was the first day of Aditi's clinical posting and she was late.

"You may remain outside. Come tomorrow on time," the JR (junior resident) said.

"But sir…," Aditi tried to explain why she was late but he didn't care to listen to her.

She came outside of the department murmuring. She was still pissed at Vaibhav but it was kind of a ritual for her to tell Vaibhav everything, so she called him.

Vaibhav saw his phone flashing "Aditi calling".

He picked up the phone and whispered, "What happened?"

She told him that she got herself out of the department on the first day by being late.

Vaibhav said, "It's okay. Don't worry, you can start from tomorrow and I know you will eventually convince them that you are a sincere and hard-working student. Now, I am hanging up otherwise I would also have to join you." And he hung up the phone.

The next day Aditi was already in the department when JR entered.

"You are before time," JR said.

Aditi wished him a "Good morning" and apologised for being late yesterday.

JR asked some introductory questions like where she belonged and schooling and stuff like that. By the time other students also arrived along with the SR (senior resident).

Aditi used to come early every day. This time she was alone in the department and busy with her book. Aashvith (JR) came and she stood up. He asked her to sit and perched himself on the table.

"Are you single?" He asked without any hesitation.

Aditi was stunned to hear the question but managed to look okay with it.

"Kind of." She replied confusingly.

"And that would mean?" Aashvith asked, raising his eyebrows and squinting his eyes.

"Yes! I am single," Aditi said, keeping in mind the recent events.

"Would you like to go out with me sometime? I mean… I would like to know you better. Here is my number, just text me if you are up for it." He wrote his number on the notepad lying next to Aditi's book and left.

Same Day At The Cafeteria During Lunch

"Hi," Vaibhav put his apron on the chair.

"Hi," Aditi replied.

"You look restless, anything wrong?" Vaibhav asked.

"Aashvith sir asked me out on a date."

Vaibhav's expression changed instantly.

"Oh! So, what are you going to do?" Vaibhav asked, sipping his tea.

"You tell me. What do you think about this situation?" Aditi countered.

Vaibhav got pissed off a little and said, "Oh! Do you want me to tell you what to do?"

"No. I mean, we should sit and talk about where we stand in our relationship to get a clear vision of what to do in the future," Aditi expressed herself.

"Look! If you are considering going out with him then we stand nowhere," Vaibhav asserted.

"What do you think? Girls don't hit on me? But I never raised a question to you about what should be done about it. It's meaningless and you are deliberately trying to imply that other people are interested in you," Vaibhav said.

"Why are you behaving so aggressively? I tell you everything and I wanted to know where we stand," Aditi explained.

"If you are confused about what our relationship is, then we stand nowhere, go out on a date with him. I don't care," Vaibhav asserted.

"How can you say that? It's high time that we define our relationship," Aditi argued.

"But this is not the way to do it. You are demeaning our relationship by asking me whether you should go on a date with another person or not," Vaibhav said, infuriated.

Aditi was freaked out and Vaibhav was furious. He had never been this angry at her before.

"So, you don't care if I date other guys?" Aditi asked, she was pissed off badly.

"If you think so, then I don't."

"You are frustrated and you are making me frustrated too," Aditi shouted.

"Oh! Then go. Make your life more happening. I won't plead in front of you to not go," Vaibhav shouted back.

Everybody in the cafeteria looked at them.

Vaibhav picked up his apron and stormed out without looking at her for a second.

Aditi felt wronged about her hopes. She had expected Vaibhav to understand her point of taking their relationship a notch up but it had gone the opposite.

They didn't exchange any messages or calls for two days.

At Girls' Hostel

Aditi searched "Aashvith" on Instagram and followed him. He instantly followed her back.

"Hi." A message popped up on Instagram chat.

"Hi, sir."

"So,"

"When?" Aditi asked.

"Coming Saturday?" Aashvith suggested.

"Sure,"

"I'll pick you up," Aashvith suggested.

"Hmm"

"Good night."

"Good night, sir"

Aditi said yes to going out with Aashvith. But she was not sure whether she will be able to pull it off or not. She couldn't sleep properly that night and brooded over the consequences of her decision of dating someone else.

Vaibhav and Aditi didn't talk to each other at college, neither during lectures nor during lunch hours or over the phone.

It was very difficult to know what was going on inside Vaibhav's mind as he was a very serious and inexpressive kind of guy, who would look the same in every situation.

On Saturday

Aditi got dressed up for her outing with Aashvith and he came to pick her up sharp at 7 pm.

They decided to go for dinner at some posh restaurant.

"You are looking gorgeous," Aashvith complimented her.

"Thank you, sir."

"We are not in college. You can drop the 'sir'," He winked.

She smiled.

"Where are we going?" She asked.

"There is this fancy place that my friends told me about. Let's check out that place."

"What kind of music do you like?" He asked.

"Good one… Hindi or English… Old or new… It doesn't matter but it should be pleasant to ears," Aditi asserted.

"Okay," he put the music on.

After a few minutes, they reached the restaurant and got seated. Aashvith had already reserved a table for them.

"Tell me about yourself." Aashvith tried to start a conversation but Aditi was quite silent and it felt like she was not in the current moment.

Aditi gave straight answers to what he was asking and didn't make any effort to make the conversation grow interesting. It was like a viva.

After a few minutes, Aashvith looked into her eyes and asked, "What's his name?"

"I didn't understand," Aditi got nervous.

"You did," Aashvith asserted.

"I am sorry. I can't focus." She stopped saying anything.

"Don't feel bad. It happens." Aashvith tried to make her comfortable.

"Now, since I do not have any chance. It hurts saying so." He touched his heart and winced.

"I should at least help you," He said.

"He is my batchmate and we are going through a rough patch in our so-called relationship," She looked sad.

"Hmm. Like what precisely?" Aashvith showed interest to know about them.

Aditi narrated everything from the beginning, all about his impassiveness and the tentative reason behind it, his insecurities and everything.

"He is so lucky. I envy him, yaar. But he must be a gem of a person to be able to make a girl like you fall for him or he is just fortunate," Aashvith said.

Aditi said, "He is one of his kind and I like him very much."

"No! You don't." Aashvith asserted.

"What does that mean?" Aditi looked confused.

"You do not only like him, you love him." Aashvith asserted.

Aditi got so bewildered that she couldn't say anything but she also knew deep down in her heart that she was insanely in love with Vaibhav.

"Give me his number," Aashvith took out his cell phone.

Aditi wondered what Aashvith was up to but she gave the number as he was her senior. Aashvith called Vaibhav and asked him to join them and sent him the address.

Vaibhav was surprised, confused and relieved all at the same time. He took 45 minutes to reach that place and those 45 minutes were filled with thrill and excitement as if he was going to see her for the first time.

Vaibhav entered the place, spotted them and approached.

"Hey! It's nice to see you, the man of the moment," Aashvith got up and invited Vaibhav to join them.

Vaibhav didn't look at Aditi at all while he was talking to Aashvith.

"Sir! I was stunned when I got your call," Vaibhav said to Aashvith.

"I called you for a reason. Since I am your senior, I am more experienced than you both in every way. The moment she got into my car and we started to talk, I knew there and then that I have no scope here. But men are men. I persuaded myself that I can charm her, but I failed.

I saw relationships shattering right in front of me just because of insecurities or ego despite being in love. Now when I look at those people, it feels as if a part of them is lost.

I am telling you both all these things because I thought I should do my bit to salvage a beautiful relationship from getting sabotaged. " Aashvith explained and got up.

"Enjoy your dinner." He left.

Vaibhav finally looked at Aditi and said in a teasing way, "You are quite dressed up."

"Not again," Aditi was still upset.

"It was hard for me too." Vaibhav's eyes glimmered with affection.

Aditi didn't utter a word. She was sad about what happened between them.

"Look, Aditi. You are precious to me more than anything in this world. It's just that I want to settle a few things in my life and then focus on us, like 200 percent. You do not deserve anything mediocre. You should realise your worth. I am lucky to have you. I want to be the best version of myself for you in every aspect. And that's the reason I never tried to take our relationship a notch higher. And after all, I am the grumpy grandpa." He joked about himself.

He wiped off a teardrop rolling down her eye and said, "I am sorry."

"You should be," Aditi said, controlling her emotions.

While they were deeply engrossed in reviving things up, the waiter kept on coming and asking them to place an order.

"We can save it for later. Let's order dinner," Vaibhav said to Aditi.

"This place looks expensive. Let's go somewhere else," Aditi whispered.

"No! You are wearing a designer dress. Let's dine here only. Don't worry! I have started doing freelance teaching and I get paid hourly," Vaibhav said while grinning into the menu and sipping water.

"Oh! So, that's what you remain busy with!" Aditi said surprisingly.

"AIIMS Delhi is a big tag. They pay me a handsome amount for teaching online. I am liking it. Now I can take my girlfriend to an expensive restaurant," Vaibhav said with pride.

Aditi was glad to hear the word 'girlfriend'. But she refrained from reacting to it as she didn't want to jinx it.

Chapter – 6

Where people start acting like couples after a few dates only, Vaibhav and Aditi took three years to reach a point where they can address themselves as a couple. Things between them were different now as Aditi was sure that Vaibhav was totally into this relationship irrespective of the time he needed to hasten up things among them.

Now they were officially going on dates.

Vaibhav curtailed the time of his freelance teaching as he was in his fourth year and he had to give time to his studies as well. But he managed to make good enough to join his friends for outings, parties and gifts and all that stuff.

At Cafeteria

"The date for my sister's wedding is fixed," Vaibhav informed everyone.

"Congratulations to her and the family," Priya said.

"Thanks! You all have to come for the wedding," Vaibhav invited them.

"Date has been fixed keeping in mind my availability to attend all the functions," Vaibhav explained.

"That's great. Otherwise, it wouldn't be possible for us to go," Aditi said.

"I can't join you guys for the wedding as I have to go home during those days for something important," Priya told them.

"What can be more important than his sister's wedding?" Prateek asked Priya.

"There is something," Priya answered, avoiding eye contact.

"Okay! No problem. You and Aditi can come together on the wedding day. I have to be there two days before you guys," Vaibhav said to Prateek.

"No problem, sir. We will join you on the day of the wedding," Aditi stated with joy.

At Vaibhav's home

All his family members, mother, sisters and father were sitting together in the drawing room when his father said, "Prashant is a nice guy. But his family, I do not trust his elder brother. He seems like a miscreant."

"Then how is Didi going to put up with the family?" Vaibhav was worried and concerned.

"She will. She is very resilient and accommodating. Prashant earns well and has no bad habits of drinking alcohol or smoking or anything of that sort." Vaibhav's father tried to reason.

Listening to his father, images of himself having tequila shots and smoking weed flashed in front of Vaibhav. But he ignored them and said, "Don't worry, Papa. Once I get settled after my medical degree, I will take care of everything."

"God bless you, son. I have had high hopes for you since always." Father said with contentment.

Vaibhav nodded with respect.

On The Day Of The Wedding

Vaibhav's home was jam-packed with relatives and he was swamped with wedding preparations, looking after decorations, settling guests, attending calls, arrangements at the venue. Amidst all this chaos, Aditi appeared in front of him in a yellow salwar suit and his heart skipped a beat but instantly he shifted his gaze toward Prateek. He asked his younger sister, Shreya, to attend Aditi.

Every eyeball turned towards Aditi. She smiled looking at them but got quite nervous with their attention as she crossed the hall and went into the room.

"Please send Vaibhav in," Aditi asked Shreya.

"He is with Prateek Bhaiya getting the luggage," Shreya answered.

Aditi perched herself on a chair after removing the pile of clothes lying on that chair.

Somebody was at the door. It was Shilpa. Aditi got up to see her and they hugged each other.

"Congratulations, Didi."

"Thanks! I am glad you came," Shilpa expressed gratitude.

"Why wouldn't I? We are family," Aditi proclaimed.

Everybody outside was talking about Aditi only but suddenly the buzzing stopped as Vaibhav and Prateek entered the hall and went to the room where Aditi was.

Door opened.

"Finally!" Aditi exhaled deeply looking at Vaibhav.

Vaibhav smiled a little looking at her.

"Didi ask someone to get some snacks for her," Vaibhav asked his sister.

"Don't worry! I will take care of her," Shilpa replied.

"It's your day, you should take some rest. I will take care of myself," Aditi said to Shilpa.

"I surely will," Shilpa said and called out for someone to get the needful done.

As soon as Shilpa left the room, "You look like Dhokla," Vaibhav teased Aditi.

Aditi frowned and hit him with her handbag. They were kidding around when Prateek taunted, "Am I invisible?" Both Aditi and Vaibhav hugged him as they ignored him. All three of them laughed out loud.

Later That Evening

Aditi wore a light apple green coloured saree and she was looking ethereal in that ensemble. She knew that it was difficult to fetch a compliment from Vaibhav but still she hoped for one. She ambled up to him and as he was about to say something someone called out his name and he left in haste.

Vaibhav and his whole family were so happy to see Shilpa as a bride. She looked gorgeous in that red attire. Preparations for other rituals began with great zeal.

A few minutes later Vaibhav saw his father and groom's brother arguing over something. His father looked tense. Vaibhav went up there and Aditi and Prateek followed him.

"You cannot ask for more at the last moment," Vaibhav's father was saying.

"This was the demand from day one. I am not adding up anything. Do you want to get your daughter married for free?" Prashant's brother said.

Vaibhav couldn't digest his tone and said, "Mind your tongue. Show some sort of respect. He is your father's age."

"Oh! Now you also have a say in this. Where were you earlier? You all have to fulfil all our demands as decided earlier or else I am afraid this marriage would be called off," Prashant's brother shouted.

Vaibhav's father said, "See, I did my best and as far as I remember, I succeeded in meeting your demands. Now if you ask me for more, I don't have any spare money left with me. So, please let things run smoothly."

"If you don't have money, ask your son. He has a whole diamond mine with him," Prashant's brother said while pointing toward Aditi.

Vaibhav got enraged and grabbed his collar, "How dare you mention her? Be within your limits." Vaibhav couldn't take it anymore.

"Vaibhav Leave him! Don't you have any affection for your sister?" His father tried to calm him down.

Prateek and Aditi pulled him apart and took him away from Prashant's brother.

"How can your son do this to the groom's brother? I assure you this insult would not be taken lightly and you will pay the price for it." Prashant's brother shouted in anger.

Family members and relatives were now drawn to the noise and marched forward to look into the matter. The wedding function turned into chaos.

Aditi couldn't muster the courage to talk to Vaibhav as she never saw him this angry before. Vaibhav walked into an empty room at the wedding venue. Aditi and Prateek followed him but stopped outside the door only.

"What should we do?" asked Aditi to Prateek.

"I have no idea," Prateek whispered.

"I think you should go inside alone but after a few minutes. Let him calm down a little," Prateek suggested.

Aditi nodded.

She peeked inside the room and saw that Vaibhav was sitting on the bed with his sleeves rolled up. Fresh sweat was shining on his face; facial muscles were taut and veins pumped up.

She entered the room and stood by his side.

"Do you see what kind of society I belong to? These people have filthy minds. I don't want to drag you into this. It's suffocating that I cannot save my sister from these wolves that can go any low for money. But at least I can save you from becoming a part of this. I hope you understand what I am saying," Vaibhav expressed his anxiety.

Aditi squatted down in front of him and put her hands on his knees, looking at him. But he was not looking at her.

"These kinds of people are in every society. The only difference is that in the society, to which I belong, people ask for money in a sophisticated manner, wearing designer suits and the amount of money is exponentially more. Every social stratum has both good and bad people. Why do you always forget that you will be a successful surgeon or physician one day? You don't know your worth and the society you belong to has nothing to do with us. I love you and I always will." Aditi expressed her profound love for him with utmost ease.

Vaibhav's eyes were wet. He took her hands into his hands, looked into her eyes and said, "I love you too. I don't know what I have done to deserve someone like you."

Their perfect romantic moment's timing was really bad. They reminded themselves that they are in the middle of a tough situation here and they got up. They were just about to leave the room and go across the door when Vaibhav pulled her by her arm and kissed her, oblivious to the time and situation which were odd.

However, after their perfect moment of love, emotion and passion they got back to their senses and

Aditi convinced him to say sorry to the groom's brother for the sake of Shilpa. Vaibhav wanted to call off the wedding at first but then he remembered what his father said about Prashant's nature.

Eventually, the matter was resolved after Vaibhav apologised for his behaviour even if he did the right thing. But he had to do that for his sister. And all the family members and relatives succeeded in persuading the groom's brother to let go of the demand for more dowry.

Aditi and Vaibhav had the best moment of their relationship at the wedding at Vaibhav's sister's wedding. Thanks to Prashant's brother.

Amidst a load of studies and clinical postings and seminars in their fourth year, their romance rose with full vigour. They were again the hot topic among the students and were part of every hostel room discussion.

All the seniors and batchmates and even juniors who had hoped to woo Aditi got disheartened.

Chapter – 7

A Regular Day

Prateek – You guys should start paying rent to my brother as half of the time you both are there only for your so-called group study.

Both Vaibhav and Aditi laughed out loud.

Vaibhav – Hey!

Aditi – Yeah! I am all ears.

Vaibhav – Would you like to move in together?

Aditi rose from her chair in excitement. She didn't want to squander away the chance of living together before Vaibhav could overthink it.

Aditi – Seriously, listening to this from you is overwhelming. I am falling short of words to explain how I feel right now.

Vaibhav – I didn't know you were this desperate.

Aditi – You kissed me after three years of being together. Who would be desperate if not me?

She smirked.

Aditi – I am all in. Let's start hunting for a place.

Vaibhav – Look, I don't have time to hunt for a place. I have to do my freelance teaching also. I know some guys; they will do it. If you like the place then we are good, because I don't have a call in this.

Aditi – Done!

Prateek – You stole my roommate.

Aditi – You shouldn't have brought up that rent thing. Your mistake.

Aditi put her arms around Vaibhav's neck and kissed him on the cheek.

Later That Week

Finally, Aditi liked one apartment after rejecting at least ten of them.

"Thanks! I thought I have to find a place on the moon to live with you," Vaibhav jokes.

Aditi ignored what Vaibhav said. Her face was lit up. She was happy and was busy envisioning her life with him.

"You get the formalities done and I shall start shopping," Aditi said excitedly.

"I am already scared looking at you so delighted," Vaibhav quipped.

"Shut up! Happiness won't kill you," Aditi hit him lightly.

After the legal formalities were done, Vaibhav and Aditi moved in. The real struggle began after that.

At The Mall

"Why are we buying so many mugs for two people?" Vaibhav asked. He was visibly irritated.

"Our friends might come someday. My family can visit us. Your family can come over. We should be prepared," Aditi said assertively as she kept on looking at the stuff.

"Family? Seriously? What have I got myself into?" Vaibhav winced.

"Just choose one. It's just a curtain. You are not going to wear it," Vaibhav said irritably.

"It should go with the furniture and walls. Just wait for a few more minutes," Aditi asked him.

Vaibhav breathed deeply and looked at his watch.

After half an hour, Aditi said, "We are done for today."

"What? That means we have to come again," Vaibhav replied while making a strange face.

"Why are you making a big deal out of this?" Aditi frowned.

"Nothing. Just get out of here. I will collapse if I spend a few more minutes here." Vaibhav was infuriated and was moving with great celerity.

"What?" Aditi said, almost running to catch up with him.

"Nothing. Just keep moving." Vaibhav said.

In The Cab

"I am exhausted as hell," Vaibhav complained.

"I am the one who did the shopping and you got exhausted, great!" Aditi bayed.

"Who was holding all the bags?" Vaibhav argued.

"Guys would be ready to compete with each other to hold my bags," Aditi winked.

"Oh! I get it." Vaibhav winced.

At Their New Apartment

Vaibhav was busy setting his study table. Aditi extended a mug in her hand toward him.

"You made tea for me!" Vaibhav said with a big smile on his face.

"Yes, for holding my bags." She said, raising her eyebrows.

"Okay! But you should have asked me what I want as my fees for holding your bags." He winked.

"I can also fire you from the job." She replied with a twinkle in her eyes.

"Wait, I'll show you." They dodged around the whole apartment and then sat on the floor catching their breath and laughing hard for at least 5 minutes.

"I am loving this, you and me. I didn't want to say it though because I don't want to jinx it," Aditi said on a serious note.

"Don't worry! No one can jinx it." Vaibhav wrapped his arms around her.

She leaned over him.

"Your tea must have gotten cold," Aditi said, getting up.

Vaibhav also rose from the floor.

At The College

"Here come our love birds," Prateek commented on the new couple.

Vaibhav and Prateek patted each other's back for a reason only they knew.

"When are you guys throwing a housewarming party?" Prateek asked.

"We just moved in and we didn't buy a house for ourselves. We are only renting it." Aditi gave an excuse.

"Whatever! There should be a celebration," Prateek asserted.

"We are planning to get a bike, after that." Aditi answered.

"Bike? Get a small car instead," Prateek suggested.

Vaibhav looked at him angrily.

"What's the problem? You can be her driver." Prateek laughed at his joke.

Everyone smiled and they didn't pull off this topic further.

Same Day In The Evening

Aditi handed Vaibhav a cup of tea and sat with her book on the floor leaning against the sofa.

While she was engrossed in her book, Vaibhav was calculating something on the paper.

"We can," Vaibhav said, still scribbling on the paper.

"What do you mean?" Aditi asked without shifting her gaze from her book.

"I can pay half of the EMI if you do the down payment. Since we will start getting paid a fair amount in the internship, I will pay you back half of the down payment," Vaibhav suggested with contentment evident on his face.

Aditi looked up at him with surprise and said, "Are you the same Vaibhav, the one who wouldn't let me buy a gift for him?"

"Love changes you as a person. Rather, love makes you a better person." Vaibhav looked at her with affection.

Aditi smiled.

"A car will save my girlfriends' hair and skin from pollution also." Vaibhav winked.

Aditi stood up and hugged him.

The same evening Aditi's mother called. After the regular greetings and knowing each other's well-being, Aditi told her mother about her current living arrangement. Since they were going to buy a car together, it was high time she spilled the beans at her home.

"He is so intelligent and diligent also. He is the only one from our batch who is earning," Aditi said to her mother.

"Should I tell your father that you are living with him?" Her mother asked on a serious note.

"I am not sure how Dad and Bhai will react after coming to know this." Aditi expressed her confusion about telling her father about Vaibhav or not.

"I am 200 percent sure about Vaibhav and eventually Dad has to know about it, so, why not know? And I know you can handle it, Mom," Aditi concluded that telling her father about her relationship was the right thing to do.

"I'll try my best, I trust you. If you are sure you are doing the right thing, I am always there for you." Aditi's mother expressed her support.

"Love you, Mom. You are the best." Aditi kissed her on the phone.

"Love you too, sweetie."

A Few Days Later

"Prateek and Priya are coming for a night's stay. Do we need to get anything from the market? Tell me beforehand. I will not go outside at the eleventh hour as you always ask me to do so," Vaibhav asked.

"Aww. Someone has become so responsible," Aditi said in her baby voice.

"See? Now, this is also a problem." You are not happy either way, Vaibhav sighed. Aditi clung to him and said, "Not at all."

The doorbell rang.

"It must be Prateek and Priya." Vaibhav went to open the door.

Prateek – I hope we didn't disturb you.

Vaibhav – What do you think we do all the time? Idiot! Come inside.

Priya – Hey! You decorated the place pretty well, Aditi.

Vaibhav – I live here too. I have given my input too. What about me?

Priya – Shut up! As if I don't know you. I know how much you are into these things.

Vaibhav shrugged his shoulders.

All four of them had dinner which they cooked together and then hopped on the bed and chatted for hours.

Aditi (to Priya) – Your family knows about Prateek, right?

Priya– Yeah! But they are still looking for a match for me and if they fail to find me a match, Prateek is their backup plan. I hate them for this.

Aditi – That's gross. This just does not feel right to me.

Prateek – Because it's not. And they talk to me as if I know nothing and they are 100 percent sure about me. By the way, my family loves Priya. So, we are good. It doesn't bother us much. There was a time when I got so depressed; wondering if her family didn't find me good enough for her. But then we worked on it and it's sorted now.

Aditi – That's good, but how?

Priya – You both are like family to us, so we can tell you. As soon as we start getting paid for an internship we will marry in court. And you guys have to be there for us.

Vaibhav – So, you are getting married because you want to get married or just to teach a lesson to your family? Are you looking to assure each other that you belong together?

Priya – After I shared my family's plan with Prateek, he got insecure and that's normal. Do you remember I couldn't make it to your sister's wedding? That's because my family has put up my profile on a matrimonial site and I had to be there at home for a formal meeting with a guy's family.

Prateek– Aditi, have you told your family that you are living with him?

Aditi – Yes, my mom knows and I have told her to tell everybody else at her discretion.

Vaibhav – And my whole town knows.

Everyone cracked into laughter.

Prateek – Are you not nervous about whether her family will like you or not?

Vaibhav – I do not care whether they like me or not. She wants me and that's enough for me. The bond two people share, the comfort and the understanding which exists between them is inexplicable. How can family members decide whether I am good for her or she is good for me? It's our thing. People are on their best behaviour when they meet each other's families. What do families judge? Your material possessions, your car, a house you own, the brands you own, etc. Nobody sees what you are from within and that's impossible by the way for anyone to perceive in a few meetings.

Aditi lauded Vaibhav for saying such wise words.

Aditi – I agree. But I never knew you were so clear in your head about the importance of the reaction of my family to our relationship. I feel relieved. I thought whenever the encounter happens I will be the one handling the situation and everyone's emotions or reactions. But you are all set. I'm so glad.

Aditi hugged Vaibhav.

Priya – It's 3 in the morning.

They looked at each other's faces and without saying anything it was clear that this discussion had to end.

Prateek – I and Priya can sleep on the floor in the hall.

Vaibhav – No. We will hit the floor buddy. Let the girls sleep in the bed.

Paediatric Department, Aiims, Delhi

Aditi's phone buzzed in between a case demonstration. It was Vaibhav on the call.

"Meet me at the gate. We are getting our car today. Prateek and Priya are already here. Come soon. Bye!"

Aditi thought about how she can leave the demonstration in between and what excuse she will make to get out.

"What is it?" Aashvith whispered.

"We are getting a car, I need to visit the showroom with him," Aditi whispered.

Aashvith – Congratulations! Quite a progress.

Aditi – Help me sneak out, sir.

Aashvith (aloud) – Sir will not allow you to be here without submitting the case study.

SR – What happened, Dr. Aashvith?

Aashvith – Sir, you carry on with the demonstration. I will handle it. You may leave Aditi. Don't come without the case study.

Both of them tried hard not to smile and Aditi moved out of the department with alacrity.

All four of them reached the showroom to get the car, then went to a nearby temple to get the blessings and the day ended with laughter, happiness and joy. A happy little world they had.

A few days later

"Vaibhav do you have your family photograph with all your family members in it," Aditi asked.

"Why?" asked Vaibhav.

"Just tell me."

"No, I don't," Vaibhav said bluntly.

Aditi made a sad baby face.

Seeing her, Vaibhav asked, "Come on, tell me why you need that."

"See we live together and we own a car together. I wanted to decorate our living room and I have my family portrait with me. So, I wanted yours too just to make this place more homely," Aditi explained.

"You can place only your family's photograph on the wall. I have no issue," Vaibhav said.

"But I have, If you don't have a family photograph, get individual photos. I'll get them framed together. Ask your sister to send the pictures, please." Aditi insisted.

She clung to him.

"No cuddling while I'm studying. Don't break the rule. I will ask my sister to send the pictures," Vaibhav stated.

Aditi and Vaibhav were living a life no less than a dream, with perfect grades, super bonding, and compatibility and they had a bright future ahead of them.

But not to forget, nothing is permanent in this world, everything has a shelf life.

Their 5th year and internship went smoothly and both of them started preparations for the forthcoming PG exams. The date of convocation was also declared. And Vaibhav was going to be felicitated with the gold medal as he topped for five years consecutively. Aditi was happier than Vaibhav about this achievement. She knew how hard he worked to manage his online teaching job, studies and his relationship. He had never complained about anything and tried his best to make everyone happy.

Chapter - 8

For parents, nothing can be more special than seeing their children in those black gowns. The feeling cannot be expressed in words. The same was the case with Vaibhav's father. He was never happier. He had called every relative and friend of his and told them about his son's achievement. He told his wife that now he will buy a new scooter for himself and will plan a trip to *Vaishno Devi* which he has always wanted to make. The glow on his face was the fruit of his patience, his son's austerity and God's grace.

Vaibhav On The Phone With His Father

Vaibhav – Yes! I have booked the train tickets. Why is the mother not coming?"

Father – She is saying she will feel out of place and uncomfortable among so many educated and big-city people.

Vaibhav – It's nothing like that. Her son will be getting a gold medal. How can she miss a chance to witness the moment?

Father – Okay! Since you have booked 2 tickets, I will try my best to convince her to come along.

Aditi calls her mother to share the news.

"We are so proud of you darling," Aditi's mother expressed her happiness.

"What about Dad? Did he say anything?" asked Aditi.

"He is happy as hell but too busy to express it." Mother clarified.

"Mom! Ask dad to be a little less flashy and boastful in front of Vaibhav and his family. I hope you understand. They are very simple and nice people," Aditi said to his mother.

"Okay! I will but you know how your father is. I cannot guarantee but I will try my best." Mother assured her.

"Is Bhai also coming?"

"Yes! He is most excited about it."

Next Day

"Aren't you happy? Our families are going to meet each other." Aditi said to Vaibhav.

"Not at all. First of all, I am only thinking about the PG exam and secondly, I am afraid of what will crop out of this meeting. I like things as they are right now."

"So, you don't want to involve our families at all. How is this possible?"

"I don't know. I haven't thought about it."

"I don't know about yours but my family is super excited to meet their future son-in-law."

They cuddled.

On The Day Of Convocation

Aditi couldn't sleep out of excitement and was up since 4:00 AM. At 6:00 AM. Vaibhav got ready to pick up his father from the railway station.

"I will see you at the ceremony. I will reach college only after picking up my father. Also, he doesn't know about us living together." Vaibhav told Aditi.

"Literally?" Aditi was surprised to know this.

"Yeah." He replied while looking for the car keys.

"Wait! I made you tea. Grab some biscuits. I have to get ready." Aditi ran into the kitchen saying this.

"Will you come with your family or should I come to pick you up?" Vaibhav asked.

"No, I will come with them."

"Fine, bye." Vaibhav kissed her on the cheek and left.

At The Ceremony

When Vaibhav was on stage receiving the gold medal, Aditi proudly told her family that he is the one with wet eyes. Vaibhav's father shed tears when he mentioned his father in his speech. It was a very emotional moment for his father as his dreams were taking the shape of reality right in front of him. Vaibhav touched his father's feet and his father hugged him like never before.

Later That Day

Aditi called Vaibhav to inform them that she and her family had been waiting in front of the cafeteria.

"Ok! We are coming right away."

Aditi was so nervous that she couldn't stand still. She was oscillating like a pendulum.

"Hey!" Vaibhav tapped Aditi's shoulder from behind.

"Namaste uncle…" Aditi greeted Vaibhav's father.

"Dad! They are here," Aditi said to her father.

Vaibhav shook hands with her brother and touched her parent's feet.

"Congratulations, beta!" Aditi's mother said to Vaibhav.

He bowed his head as a gesture of gratitude and respect. Vaibhav's father was very nervous seeing them. Aditi's father and brother also looked quite confused and dissatisfied seeing Vaibhav's father.

Aditi's family was a flashy and sophisticated Gujarati business family and Vaibhav's father was a supervisor in a factory in a town in Uttar Pradesh; the dissimilarity was striking.

"What does your factory produce, sir?" Aditi's father initiated a conversation with Vaibhav's father.

"Electric wires," Vaibhav's father replied.

Aditi felt uneasy as she knew where this conversation was heading and its outcome might be unpleasant.

"And what is the turnover on average every year?" Aditi's father further asked.

Vaibhav's father gave him the answer.

"So, do you have only this factory?" Aditi's father further asked.

Vaibhav's father, Vaibhav and Aditi were surprised by this question and looked at each other in oblivion.

"I work as a supervisor there. I do not own that factory," Vaibhav's father replied hesitatingly.

Vaibhav looked furiously at Aditi because he thought Aditi had lied to his family about his father.

Aditi looked at her mother, clueless and helpless. Aditi's father's expressions were completely changed. He said, "Why did you lie in the first place about being the owner of a factory?"

"I don't know what you are talking about." Vaibhav's father was feeling insulted.

"Then your son must have lied to my daughter," Aditi's father shouted.

Vaibhav's father looked at Vaibhav and he in turn looked at Aditi with his teeth clenched for an explanation.

"No, Dad. He never said that. You somehow misunderstood. Mom, say something!" Aditi shouted at her mom.

Her mom stood there silently as she was the one who lied about Vaibhav's father owning a factory.

"I saw his family members' picture at the apartment. Maids working at our home look better than his mother and sister," Aditi's brother remarked.

"Mind your tongue, otherwise, I will forget you're her brother," Vaibhav said angrily with his face flushed red.

"Please, brother. Stop saying such things. I beg you," Aditi said to her brother.

"He might have thought that catching a big fish might take his clan out of poverty at once," Aditi's brother said in a boastful manner.

"Aditi, how can you ruin my name by getting involved with people of such low profile? Half of Ahmedabad is waiting for Virat Shah's daughter's wedding and you want to marry him? How will I show my face to the community?" Aditi's father said to her while she was all in tears trying to stop her family from saying mean things.

"For God's sake, stop!" Aditi pleaded in front of her father and brother.

"See this man. I won't even keep him as my driver. Forget about marrying you to his son," Aditi's brother said, looking at Vaibhav's father.

Vaibhav did not take a second to punch him right in the face and soon the bickering turned into a fight. Vaibhav's batchmates and juniors came running and assaulted Aditi's brother and beat him badly.

Vaibhav just stood up when he heard the faint voice of his father calling out to him.

His hand was on his chest and he complained of chest pain. Vaibhav and his friends took him to the emergency as soon as possible.

Aditi's brother also got wounded badly and was admitted to the trauma department.

Once her brother got bandaged she ran towards the emergency department to see Vaibhav's father's situation.

Prateek stopped her in the corridor and asked her not to go inside. He told her that Vaibhav didn't want to see her.

She was all in tears and tried to convince the boys to let her go inside. But Prateek asked her to leave and avoid any unpleasant situation. She remained there standing and crying but Vaibhav didn't come outside. His friends didn't let her in.

After One And Half Hours

Aditi was there in the corridor leaning against the wall when she got to see Vaibhav's face for a second. His eyes were red and he was in tears.

She saw Prateek coming toward her.

"He lost his father to a heart attack. His father is no more. You must leave. I beg you," Prateek said.

Aditi couldn't believe her ears. She couldn't feel her legs.

"Can I talk to him once? He needs me," Aditi pleaded.

"You are the last person he needs to see right now. Please, try to understand." Prateek countered.

Prateek pulled her by arm and asked her not to come until Vaibhav was in a stable state.

Prateek had asked Priya to take her to the apartment and be with her. Aditi refused to talk to her family or see them. Vaibhav and his friends left with his father's dead body to his hometown for the last rites.

Vaibhav barely spoke anything since the moment his father passed away. A volcano of emotions erupted within him and millions of images were flashing and getting faded away. He was still in denial and was unable to accept the truth. A lot happened that day. In the morning, he had his girlfriend with him, the love of his life. In the afternoon, he had the most awaited and special moment with his father. His austerity had paid off in the form of the happy tears in his father's eyes; the moment his father was waiting for a lifetime. In the evening his love, his pride, his world, shattered right in front of his eyes.

Aditi called Vaibhav hundreds of times but to no avail. Aditi lost her sanity. She stopped eating and kept crying all the time. After 3 days Prateek and one more friend of Vaibhav came to Aditi and Vaibhav's apartment to pack his things up and send those things back to his home. Vaibhav also sent the car keys that they owned together.

Aditi asked them about Vaibhav's condition and refused to give his things. She was hoping that he would come back. But they had told her that he was not coming back.

Prateek asked Priya to call Aditi's family and to come and take her along. She was not in a condition to live there alone. The same day in the evening, Aditi's family took her back to Ahmedabad.

Their perfect dreamy relationship has ended brutally. It was something that they had never imagined. It was all because of a lie that Aditi's mother told her husband. The intent was not to hurt anyone but to evade an adverse reaction from her husband. She thought that once he meets Vaibhav, he will approve of his daughter's choice out of the love he had for her.

But she was wrong. She had failed to anticipate the consequences of that lie and everybody's life changed forever. Vaibhav had lost his father. Aditi started hating her family. Two people who were madly in love with each other fell apart.

Does love always win? Let's see.

Chapter – 9

At Aditi's Home In Ahmedabad

Aditi went into depression and needed medical intervention to be saved from the condition she was in.

"For how long would we have to endure her madness? She doesn't talk to anyone or eat properly," Aditi's brother said to his parents.

"He is right. In the coming months, Aadit's (Aditi's brother) wedding preparations will begin. How are we going to answer all the questions thrown at us? She looks miserable," the father said.

"Still! After what happened in Delhi, both of you only worried about your image in society," the mother said in disgust.

Every time Aditi looked at her phone, she hoped that Vaibhav would call and everything would be as it was. But months had passed and he didn't call or message her.

Vaibhav lost his mother a few months after his father's demise. Since his elder sister was already married, he and his younger sister were left in the family. His world had gone upside down but the one who copes with adverse situations has the potential to grow strong.

At Vaibhav's Home

The only productive work Vaibhav used to do was his freelance teaching online because he had the responsibility of his younger sister. Other times he used to sit at his study table in the name of PG preparation and would keep fidgeting with his phone. He was paradoxical about whether he should call Aditi or not. His condition was as miserable as Aditi's.

Her younger sister used to cook for him and keep it on his table and the next day she would find it as it is. He used to skip his lunch and dinner often and his health deteriorated. He started taking alcohol daily and sometimes would take his classes drunk. His sister got worried and shared the ordeal with her elder sister and her husband, Prashant.

The day the results were out of the post-graduation exam, Prateek called Vaibhav. After abusing each other, Prateek informed Vaibhav that he had secured a good rank and would get the branch of his choice. Vaibhav congratulated him and told him that he couldn't make it. Prateek was shocked to get to know that Vaibhav couldn't secure a PG seat in the post-graduation exam.

Prateek sensed that Vaibhav needed intervention and planned to visit him. Two days later, he reached Vaibhav's home. His sister had told Prateek everything about Vaibhav and how worried she was for her brother.

Door knocked.

"Who is it? Come in," Vaibhav yelled. Vaibhav almost cried seeing Prateek despite controlling his best not to.

"What are you up to my friend?" Prateek asked in a worrisome manner.

"I don't know," Vaibhav replied

"Aditi didn't appear for the exam," Prateek informed him.

Vaibhav didn't respond.

"Look, my friend. You are making both of your lives miserable. You are punishing her for a crime she has not committed. Priya told me that she is under medical supervision and is not even on talking terms with her family." Prateek held his hands and tried to make him let go of his anger toward Aditi.

After being silent for a few minutes, Vaibhav said, "I know, she hasn't done anything."

"Then why are you being so stubborn? Please talk to her. You guys belong to each other." Prateek tried to persuade him.

"My family is destroyed. My mother couldn't bear the loss and she also left us. My sister lost both her parents. And whatever I do, I cannot bring normality into her life. After all this, how can I live with Aditi? Seeing her every time will remind me of the insult inflicted upon my father by her family. I am still trapped at that moment. No matter how much I try, I'm unable to overcome it." He explained the predicament he was in.

"Then try to forget her. Be as you were before like the one I met in college. The one who took care of us like a family and was our guiding light, our inspiration," Prateek said being emotional.

"Be there for your sister, nail the post-graduation exam next year and do what your father wanted you to. I hope you are getting my point," This was the crux of Prateek's visit, to drag him on the track.

Vaibhav could only nod at this point. But he was slowly absorbing what his friend had meant.

Ahmedabad

"Would you like to come shopping with us for your brother's wedding?" Aditi's mother asked.

Aditi looked disinterested and said "NO" bluntly. Her mother sat by her side and before she could say anything Aditi stood up and left the room.

While walking in the garden at night Aditi thought that wedding festivities were starting shortly. It was there and then that she decided to work hard to secure a seat for post-graduation abroad so that she didn't have to be a part of her brother's wedding. She felt guilty for thinking this way but couldn't forgive her father. They didn't even repent of their actions. It made it harder for her to forgive them.

In the coming days, she immersed herself in books to execute what she had planned.

At Vaibhav's Home

He came out of the room and saw his elder sister and her husband there. He asked them about coming uninformed suddenly.

"Shreya is quite unwell," said Shilpa.

"What? Why didn't she tell me?" Vaibhav said confoundedly.

Vaibhav went into Shreya's room without letting their elder sister complete her sentence.

"Shreya!" He entered the room.

"What happened?" Vaibhav asked in a worried manner. He checked her temperature and asked further questions regarding her health.

"Why didn't you tell me that you are unwell?" Vaibhav asked Shreya.

She didn't reply.

"I am asking something," Vaibhav repeated the question.

Shilpa and Prashant also entered the room. Shreya looked at her sister and started crying.

"What's going on?" Vaibhav yelled.

"I am scared of you. You have started drinking during the day and I don't know. It doesn't feel like it was before," Shreya said looking at Vaibhav.

Vaibhav looked at his elder sister with wet eyes.

"I'm sorry! I let everyone down. I promise you both that I won't be like this anymore." He hugged Shreya.

"I am sorry, Shreya." Vaibhav was visibly disappointed in himself.

"Didi, you should take her along with you. She will feel better," Vaibhav said to Shilpa.

"Who will take care of you then?" Shreya said.

"Since when you became my mother, just go with Didi," Vaibhav said assertively.

"I'll not. I'll be with you." Shreya insisted.

"She is right. We cannot leave you alone," the elder sister said.

They had an emotional family moment for the first time after their parent's demise.

After Shreya was asleep. Shilpa had called Vaibhav to have a word with him.

"Why don't you talk to her if you miss her so much?" Shilpa asked.

"You know nothing," Vaibhav said.

"Then tell me." She tried to elicit a response from Vaibhav. But he remained silent. She reiterated his concern.

Vaibhav narrated everything about the day his father had a heart attack and passed away because no one at his home knew about how it happened in detail. Both of them cried their hearts out remembering their father.

"I understand why you are not willing to talk to her. But trust me, you are doing it for all the wrong reasons. What happened was destiny. No one killed our father with a dagger. He was a heart patient and had already had 2 attacks before. No one can cause anyone's death against God's will," Shilpa tried to explain.

"So, you stop being an idiot and talk to her."

"I will think about it."

Shilpa's words alleviate his pain a little and a ray of hope emerged.

Vaibhav now refrained from using alcohol and started giving time to Shreya apart from his exam preparation and online teaching.

Vaibhav's austerity was fructified when he secured a very good rank in the post-graduation exam. Things were more than normal at Vaibhav's place. He shared a good bond with her sisters and even Prashant. It was like they had finally overcome their parent's death. Vaibhav motivated Shreya to do well in her academics so that she would be independent before getting married. Shilpa and her husband also supported Vaibhav and Shreya. Their parents would have been feeling proud of their children in heaven.

And one day out of the blue, Vaibhav called Prateek and asked about Aditi's whereabouts.

Prateek told him that, through Priya, he came to know that Aditi had left the country and was settled abroad. Vaibhav thought that she might have moved on and was out of love. He was hurt deeply but he was used to having unpleasant incidents in life, this was an addition to them.

Chapter – 10

7 Years Later

At A Multispecialty Hospital, In New Delhi, 11:00 Am

"Where is the neurosurgery department?" a patient asked the ward boy. The ward boy directed the patient towards the same.

"Sir, should I send the next patient?" the attendant asked the neurosurgeon.

"Yes," the doctor replied.

The patient came in.

"Show me the MRI scan," The patient handed him the scan and the report.

"Where do you live?"

"Sir, I have a job in London. I got this MRI done there only."

The doctor's expression changed as he finished reading the report. It was signed by 'Aditi Shah', a radiologist. Millions of images flashed in front of the doctor whose name was 'Vaibhav Sinha'.

He remained silent for a few minutes and then asked the patient, "Do you have the full address and phone number of the place from where you got this MRI done?"

"Yes, I do have."

Vaibhav gave him his next appointment after doing the needful.

He kept looking at the address and phone number for quite a few minutes before he made the call and enquired about the radiologist at their hospital.

It was Aditi, his Aditi. He took the very first flight to London and reached the concerned hospital.

London

"I need to see Dr. Aditi Shah," Vaibhav stated firmly to the receptionist.

"Do you have an appointment?"

"No, I am a friend from India. Dr. Vaibhav. Tell her my name."

Vaibhav's heart was pacing at double the rate.

"She left 5 minutes before. You can see her tomorrow."

"Can I get her address?"

"Not before confirming with her." The receptionist called Aditi.

"She is not picking up the call. She must be driving."

"What's your name?"

"Stephanie."

"Look Steph, this is a matter of life and death. I need to see her. Please, help me." Vaibhav tried to convince her.

"I don't know why I am doing this. Fine, this is her address." She handed him a piece of paper.

"Steph! You are an angel. Does her husband live with her?" Vaibhav asked.

"You are saying that you are her friend and don't even know that she's not married? I am already regretting giving you her address," Stephanie said, squinting her eyes.

Vaibhav was relieved knowing that Aditi wasn't married.

"No, I promise. You won't regret it." Vaibhav smiled at her and left.

Vaibhav booked a cab. Every passing second was like a year for him. He couldn't help but imagine how Aditi was going to react after seeing him. He was desperate to see her more than ever.

Doorbell rang.

Aditi opened the door and couldn't believe her eyes. It was Vaibhav at her doorstep.

The feeling they were having; seeing each other after 7 long years was inexplicable. She stood at the door looking at him, mesmerised.

"Wouldn't you let me in?" Vaibhav asked.

She turned around and started crying but then controlled her emotions and asked him to come inside and sit.

She went into the kitchen and got 2 cups of tea.

Vaibhav saw 2 cups and said, "When did you start having tea?"

"I never stopped loving you. Neither did I stop making tea for you and since you were not around, I started drinking it myself."

"How have you been?" She asked in a dull voice.

"I have been…" Vaibhav couldn't muster up the courage and stopped.

"You know my father was a simple man. The only dream he ever saw was seeing me as a doctor. I lost him that day. I lost everything that day, my father, my love, my zest for life, ambition, everything.

For days I could not accept that it happened. I felt guilty for taking him to meet your parents that day. I felt guilty for missing you in my life because I used to think that you were the reason for those unfortunate events.

I tried everything to distract my mind from your thoughts but I failed. Alcohol, weed, nothing helped.

I wanted to see you badly, hug you, be with you and at the same time hate you. I lost my sanity and failed to do anything productive. After my mother's sudden demise it was my sister's plight that made me realise that I was drowning. It took me a year to pull myself together and start over. I did exceptionally well in the post-graduation exam after failing for the first time, opting for neurosurgery after the completion of MCH and working as one since then. I got my sister married and now I'm alone with your thoughts. I died every day not being able to be with you. My love for you overpowered my hatred for you. I am incomplete without you; null, void and a body without a soul."

Aditi heard him in silence.

He stood up and looked at the wall in her living room. He went near the wall to have a closer look. All pictures of them; from day one to the day they parted ways were on that wall. There were quotes written below some of them.

He touched them and tried to cherish and feel all those love-filled and happy moments.

"I don't have words to express how sorry I am for what you've been through. Since you never gave me a chance to explain myself, I'll do it now. I never lied about you or your family. It was…"

Vaibhav turned toward her and stopped her from explaining herself further.

"Shush!" He kept his finger on her lips.

"We suffered a lot, both of us. I don't want to go down that lane again. It was unfortunate. But it's over now," Vaibhav whispered.

They looked into each other's eyes with tears of love and Vaibhav kissed her **LIKE NEVER BEFORE.**

www.ingramcontent.com/pod-product-compliance
Lightning Source LLC
Chambersburg PA
CBHW061348160726
47995CB00001B/228